This edition published by Parragon Books Ltd in 2016 and distributed by

Parragon Inc.
440 Park Avenue South, 13th Floor
New York, NY 10016
www.parragon.com

Written by David Bedford
Illustrated by Brenna Vaughan and Henry St. Leger
Edited by Laura Baker
Designed by Alisa Cullen
Production by Rob Simenton

ISBN 978-1-4748-6275-2

Printed in China

I love my Daddy

Parragon

Bath • New York • Cologne • Melbourne • Delhi
Hong Kong • Shenzhen • Singapore

One day, Little Squirrel went out to play with his daddy. Little Squirrel wanted to show Daddy Squirrel all the things he could do.

"What should we play first?" said Daddy.

"I know," said Little Squirrel excitedly …

"Digging!
Look, Daddy!" said Little Squirrel,

as he dug
and dug
and dug,

with his little
tail wagging.

"Good job!" said Daddy.
But suddenly, Little Squirrel's
tail stopped wagging.

"Help, Daddy!"

cried Little Squirrel.

"I'm stuck!"

Daddy Squirrel helped Little
Squirrel wriggle out of the hole,
and gave him a soothing hug. "You
are a good digger!" said Daddy.

"What should we play next?"

"I know," said Little Squirrel ...

"Climbing!

Look, Daddy!" said Little Squirrel, and he climbed as high as he could go, looking around as far as he could see.

"Good job!" said Daddy.
But suddenly Little Squirrel
closed his eyes tightly …

Daddy Squirrel helped Little Squirrel climb down and gave him a soothing hug. "You are a good climber!" said Daddy. "What should we play next?"

"I know ...
Jumping!
Look, Daddy!" said Little Squirrel,

and he jumped,

and jumped,

and JUMPED

with a big smile on his
little squirrel face.

But suddenly Little Squirrel
stopped smiling, and …

Splat!

"Help, Daddy!" cried Little Squirrel. "I'm stuck again!"

Daddy Squirrel helped Little
Squirrel out of the sticky mud and
gave him a soothing hug.

"You are good
at jumping!" said Daddy.
But Little Squirrel shook
his head sadly …

"I don't want to play anymore,"
said Little Squirrel.

"I always get stuck.
I can't do **anything!**"

Daddy Squirrel lifted Little
Squirrel high on to his shoulders.
"Let's play together," he said.

"Let's run!"
cried Daddy Squirrel.

Little Squirrel held on
tightly as they whooshed
through the woods.

"Yippeee!"

he shouted.

"Let's climb!"
said Daddy Squirrel.
Little Squirrel kept his eyes
open wide as they reached
the top of a tree.

"Wheeee!" he shouted.

"And now," said Daddy Squirrel,

"let's jump!"

Splat!

"Oh, help!"
cried Daddy Squirrel.
"Now I'm stuck!"

Little Squirrel
giggled as he helped
his daddy out of the
sticky mud.

"You can do **everything**, Little Squirrel!" said Daddy proudly, as they washed their muddy paws in the stream. "You can even save a Daddy Squirrel!"

Little Squirrel climbed high on to his daddy's shoulders again. "I love playing with you, Daddy," he said. "And …"

"I love my daddy!"

shouted Little Squirrel,
as they raced home
happily together.